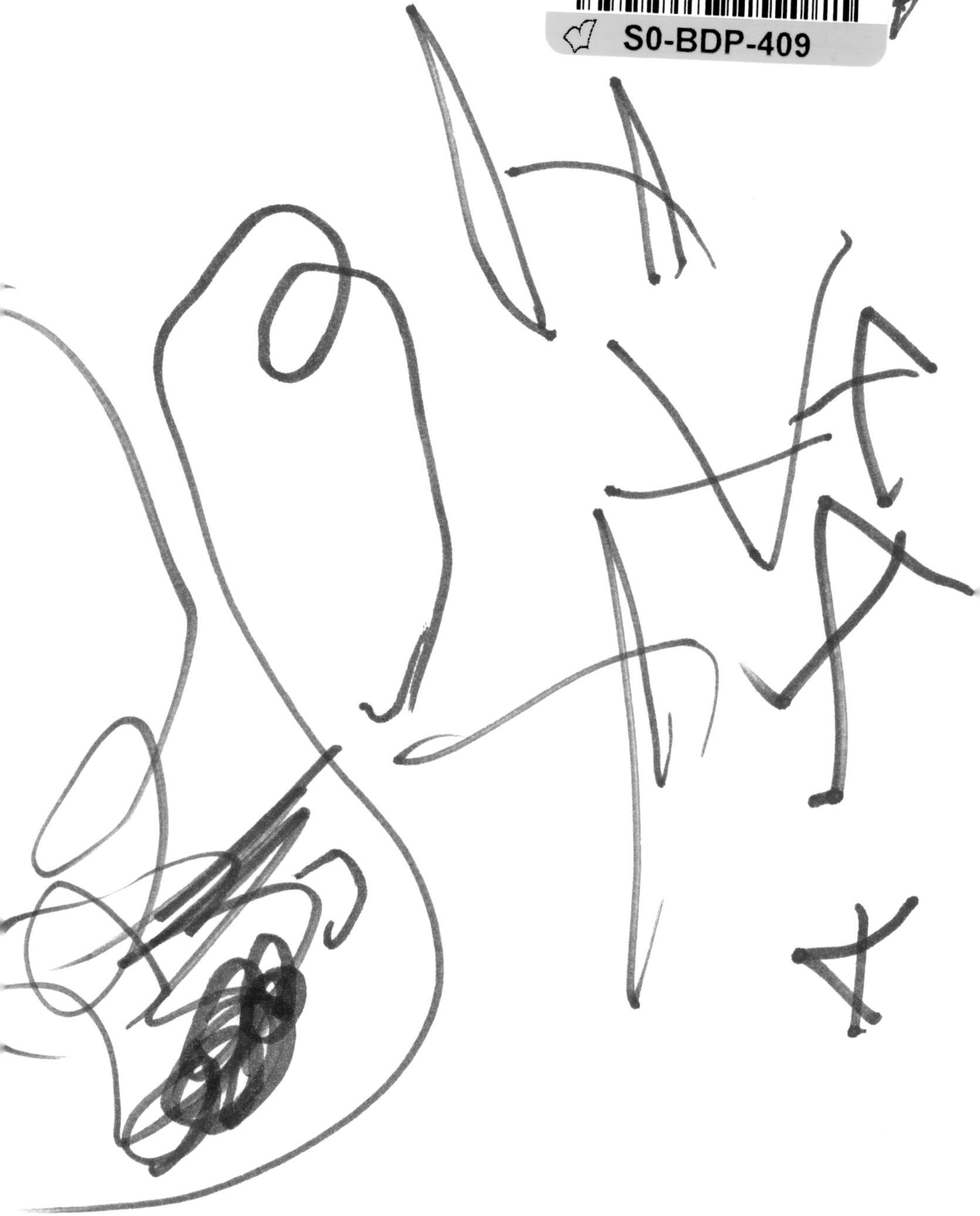

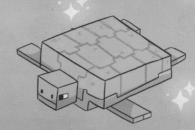

MINECRAFT™

#8

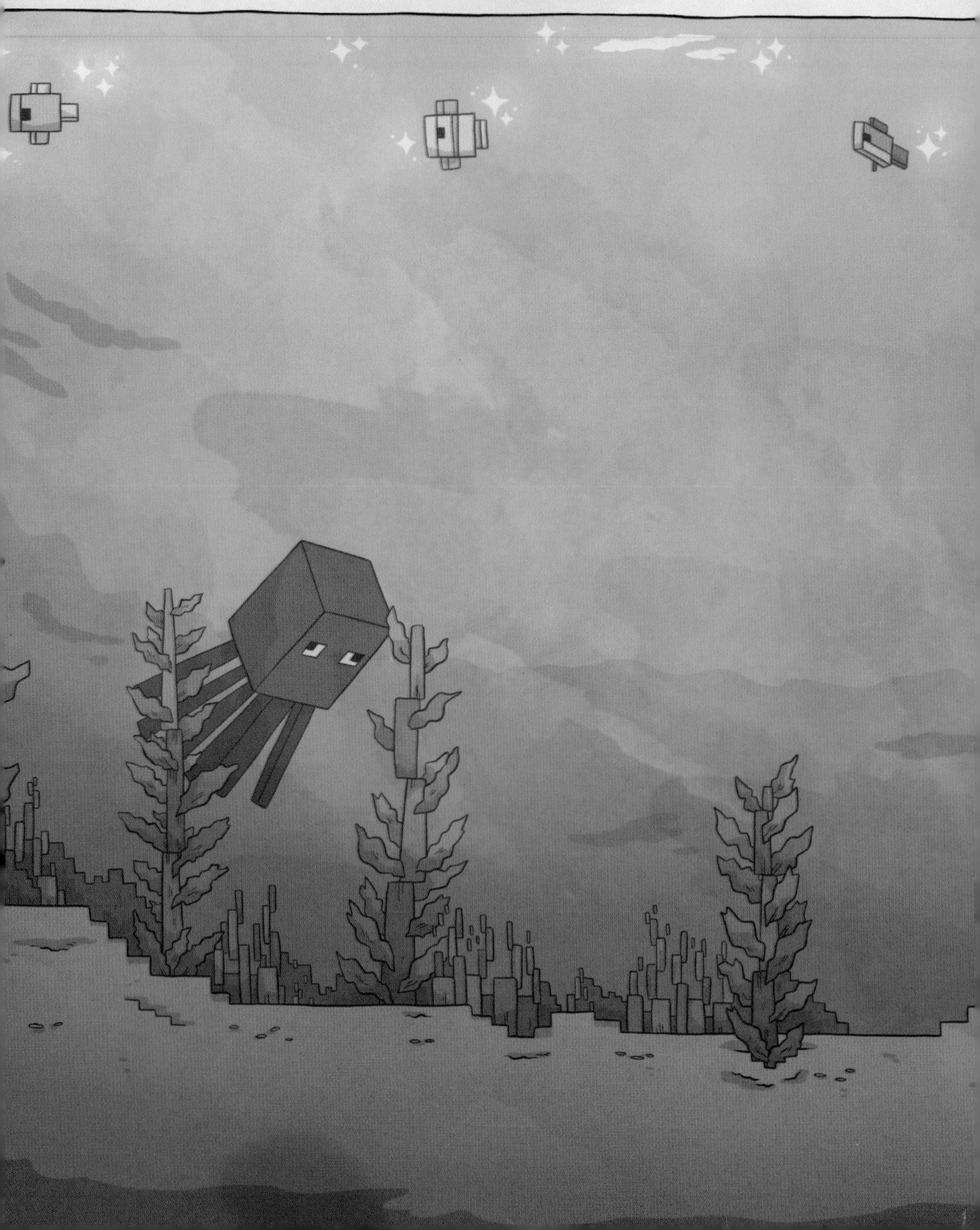

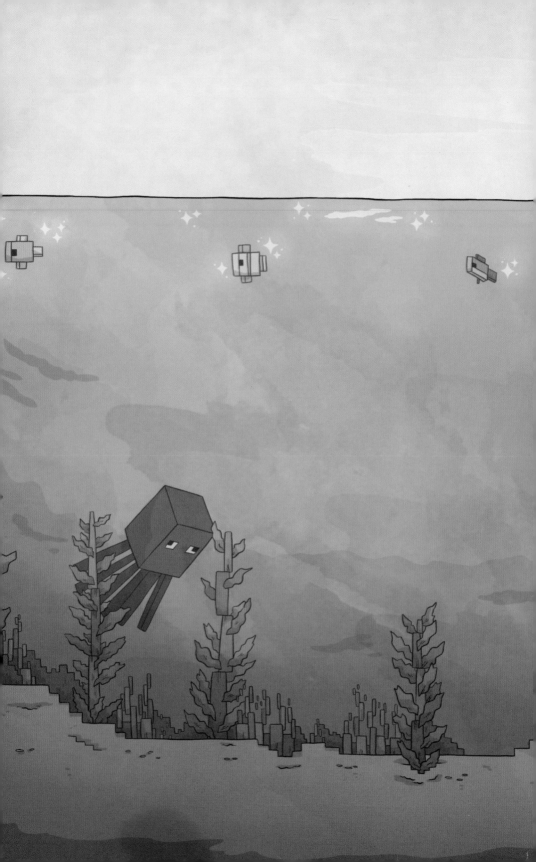

MINECRAFT™

#8

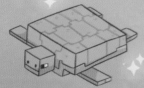

WRITTEN BY
SFÉ R. MONSTER

ART AND COVER BY
SARAH GRALEY

COLOR ASSISTANCE BY
STEF PURENINS

LETTERED BY
JOHN J. HILL

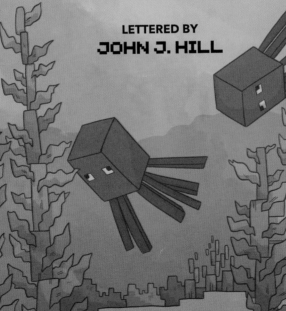

MOJANG STUDIOS

DARK HORSE BOOKS

ABDOBOOKS.COM

Reinforced library bound edition published in 2022 by Spotlight, a division of ABDO, PO Box 398166, Minneapolis, Minnesota 55439. Spotlight produces high-quality reinforced library bound editions for schools and libraries. Published by agreement with Dark Horse Comics.

Printed in the United States of America, North Mankato, Minnesota.
092021   012022

THIS BOOK CONTAINS
RECYCLED MATERIALS

Library of Congress Control Number: 2021939416

Publisher's Cataloging-in-Publication Data

Names: Monster, Sfé R., author. | Graley, Sarah; Hill, John J., illustrators.
Title: Minecraft / writer: Sfé R. Monster; art: Sarah Graley; John J. Hill.
Description: Minneapolis, Minnesota: Spotlight, 2022 | Series: Minecraft
Summary: In the world of Minecraft, a group of friends goes on countless adventures, including going on the Ultimate Quest to face off against the ender dragon and battling pirates.
Identifiers: ISBN 9781098250621 (#1, lib. bdg.) | ISBN 9781098250638 (#2, lib. bdg.) | ISBN 9781098250645 (#3, lib. bdg.) | ISBN 9781098250652 (#4, lib. bdg.) | ISBN 9781098250669 (#5, lib. bdg.) | ISBN 9781098250676 (#6, lib. bdg.) | ISBN 9781098250683 (#7, lib. bdg.) | ISBN 9781098250690 (#8, lib. bdg.)
Subjects: LCSH: Minecraft (Game)--Juvenile fiction. | Quests (Expeditions)--Juvenile fiction. | Adventure Stories--Juvenile fiction. | Dragons--Juvenile fiction. | Pirates--Juvenile fiction. | Friendship--Juvenile fiction
Classification: DDC 741.5--dc23

Spotlight

A Division of ABDO
abdobooks.com

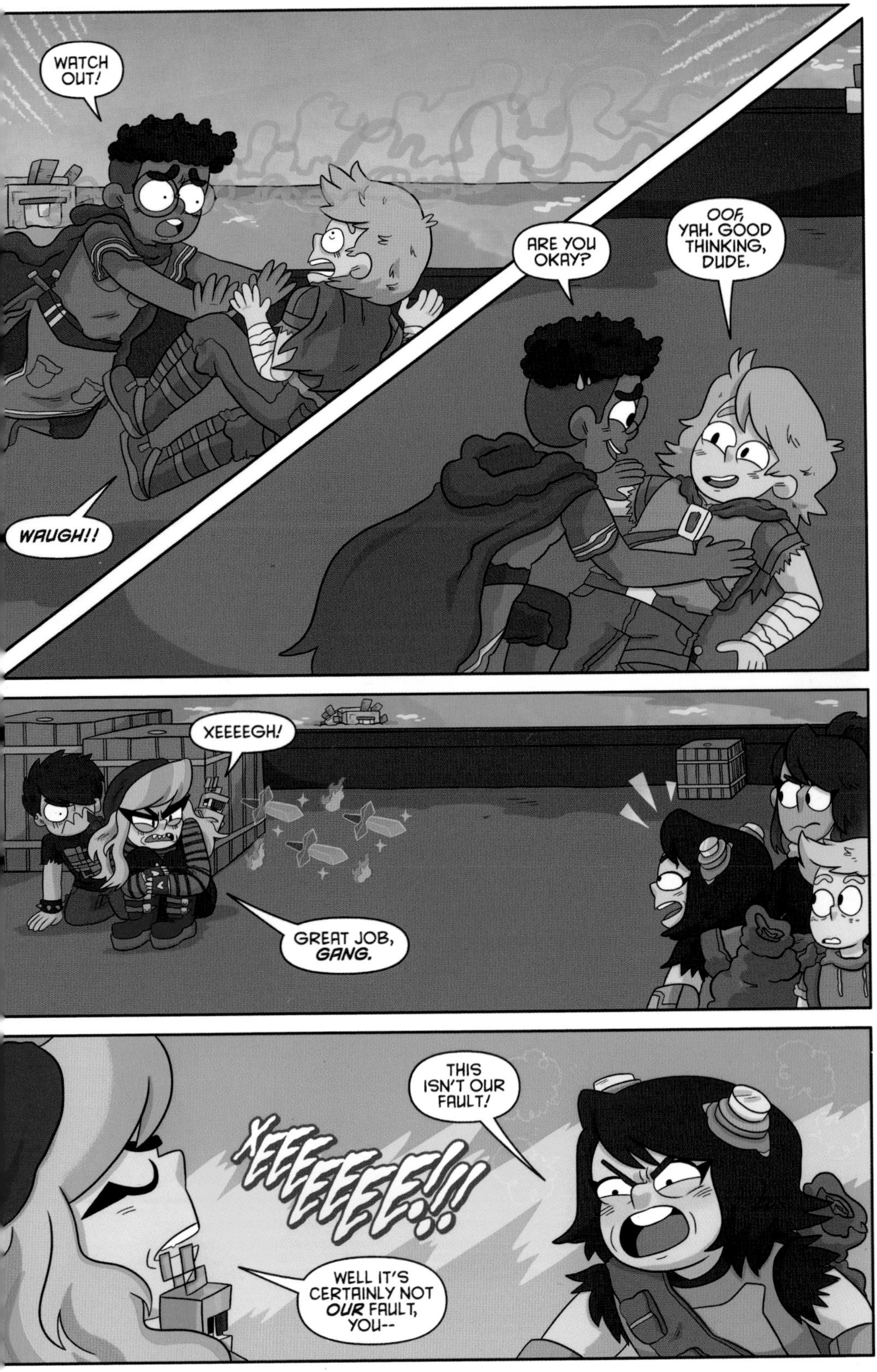
WATCH OUT!
WAUGH!!
ARE YOU OKAY?
OOF, YAH. GOOD THINKING, DUDE.
XEEEEGH!
GREAT JOB, *GANG.*
XEEEEEEE!!!
THIS ISN'T OUR FAULT!
WELL IT'S CERTAINLY NOT *OUR* FAULT, YOU--

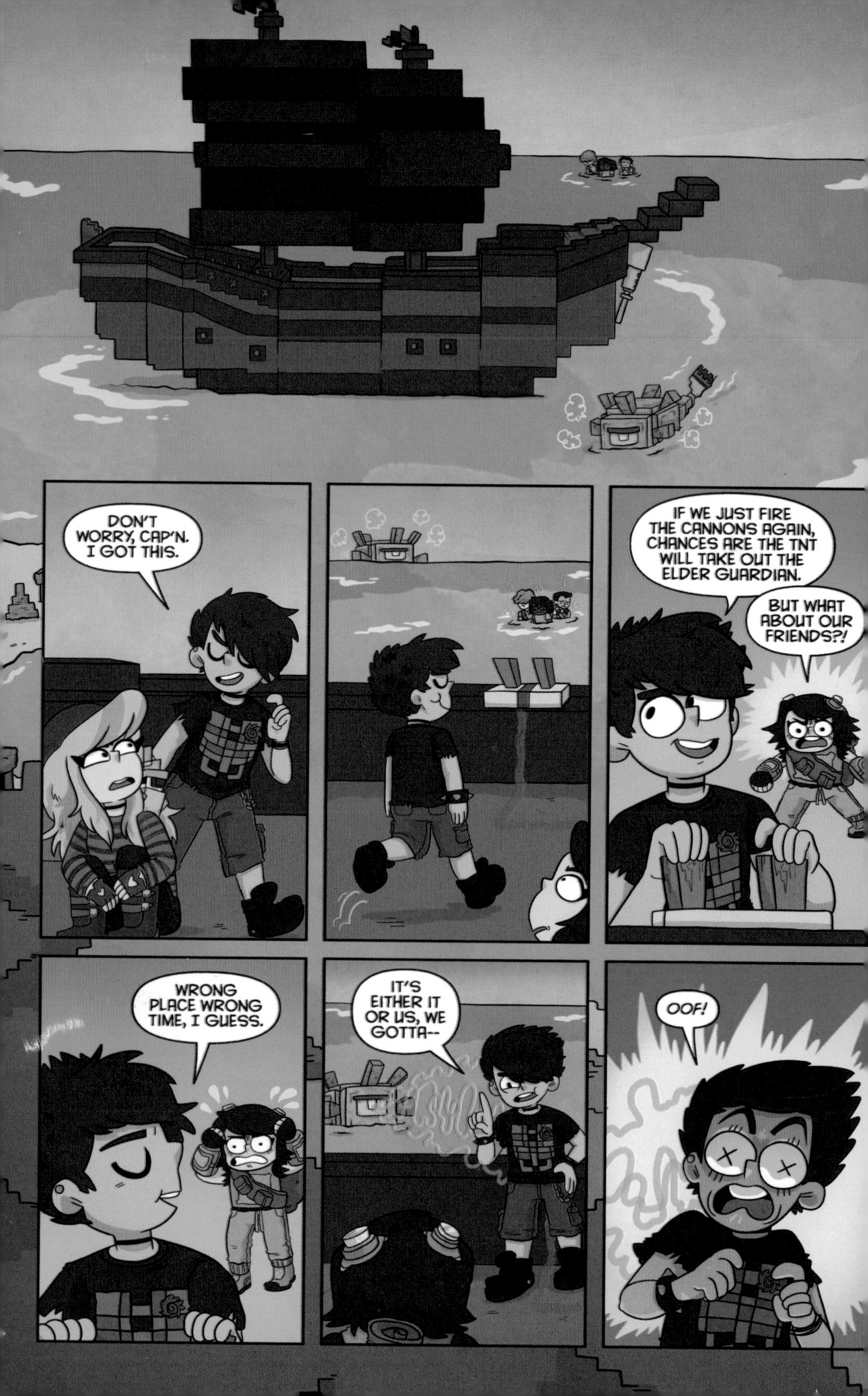
DON'T WORRY, CAP'N. I GOT THIS.
IF WE JUST FIRE THE CANNONS AGAIN, CHANCES ARE THE TNT WILL TAKE OUT THE ELDER GUARDIAN.
BUT WHAT ABOUT OUR FRIENDS?!
WRONG PLACE WRONG TIME, I GUESS.
IT'S EITHER IT OR US, WE GOTTA--
OOF!

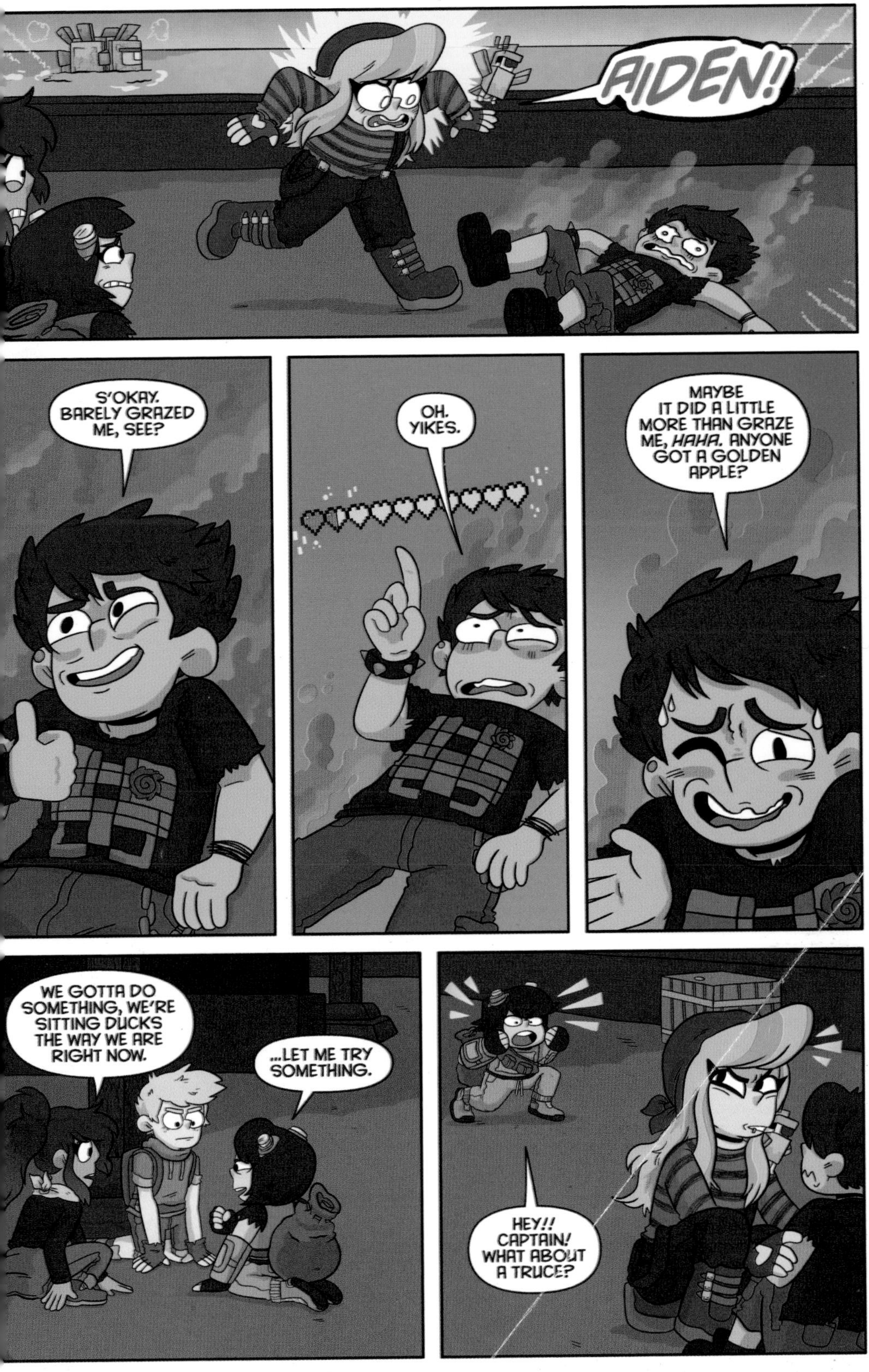
AIDEN!
S'OKAY. BARELY GRAZED ME, SEE?
OH. YIKES.
MAYBE IT DID A LITTLE MORE THAN GRAZE ME, *HAHA*. ANYONE GOT A GOLDEN APPLE?
WE GOTTA DO SOMETHING, WE'RE SITTING DUCKS THE WAY WE ARE RIGHT NOW.
...LET ME TRY SOMETHING.
HEY!! CAPTAIN! WHAT ABOUT A TRUCE?

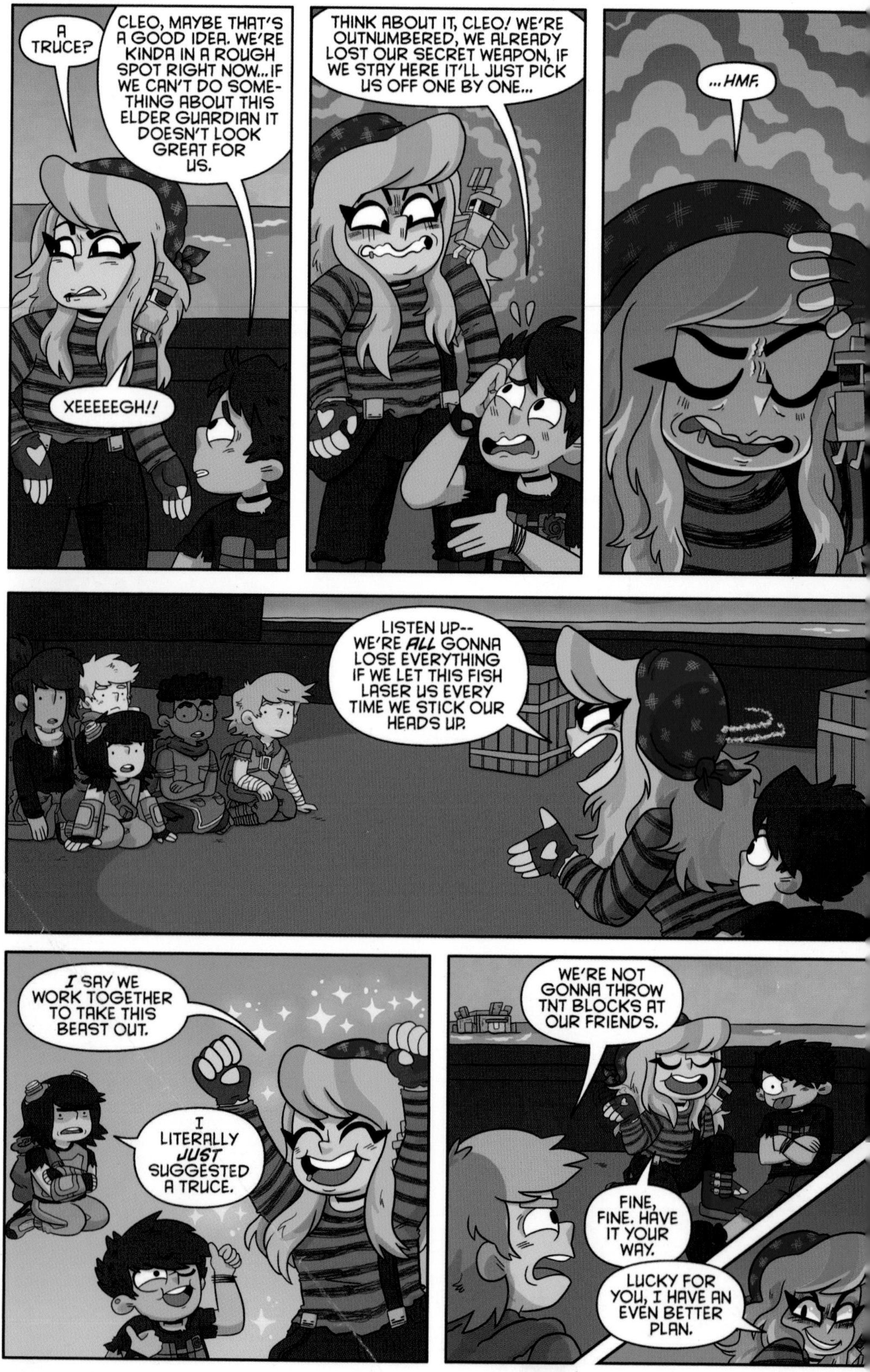
A TRUCE?
CLEO, MAYBE THAT'S A GOOD IDEA. WE'RE KINDA IN A ROUGH SPOT RIGHT NOW... IF WE CAN'T DO SOMETHING ABOUT THIS ELDER GUARDIAN IT DOESN'T LOOK GREAT FOR US.
XEEEEEGH!!
THINK ABOUT IT, CLEO! WE'RE OUTNUMBERED, WE ALREADY LOST OUR SECRET WEAPON, IF WE STAY HERE IT'LL JUST PICK US OFF ONE BY ONE...
...HMF.
LISTEN UP-- WE'RE ALL GONNA LOSE EVERYTHING IF WE LET THIS FISH LASER US EVERY TIME WE STICK OUR HEADS UP.
I SAY WE WORK TOGETHER TO TAKE THIS BEAST OUT.
I LITERALLY JUST SUGGESTED A TRUCE.
WE'RE NOT GONNA THROW TNT BLOCKS AT OUR FRIENDS.
FINE, FINE. HAVE IT YOUR WAY.
LUCKY FOR YOU, I HAVE AN EVEN BETTER PLAN.

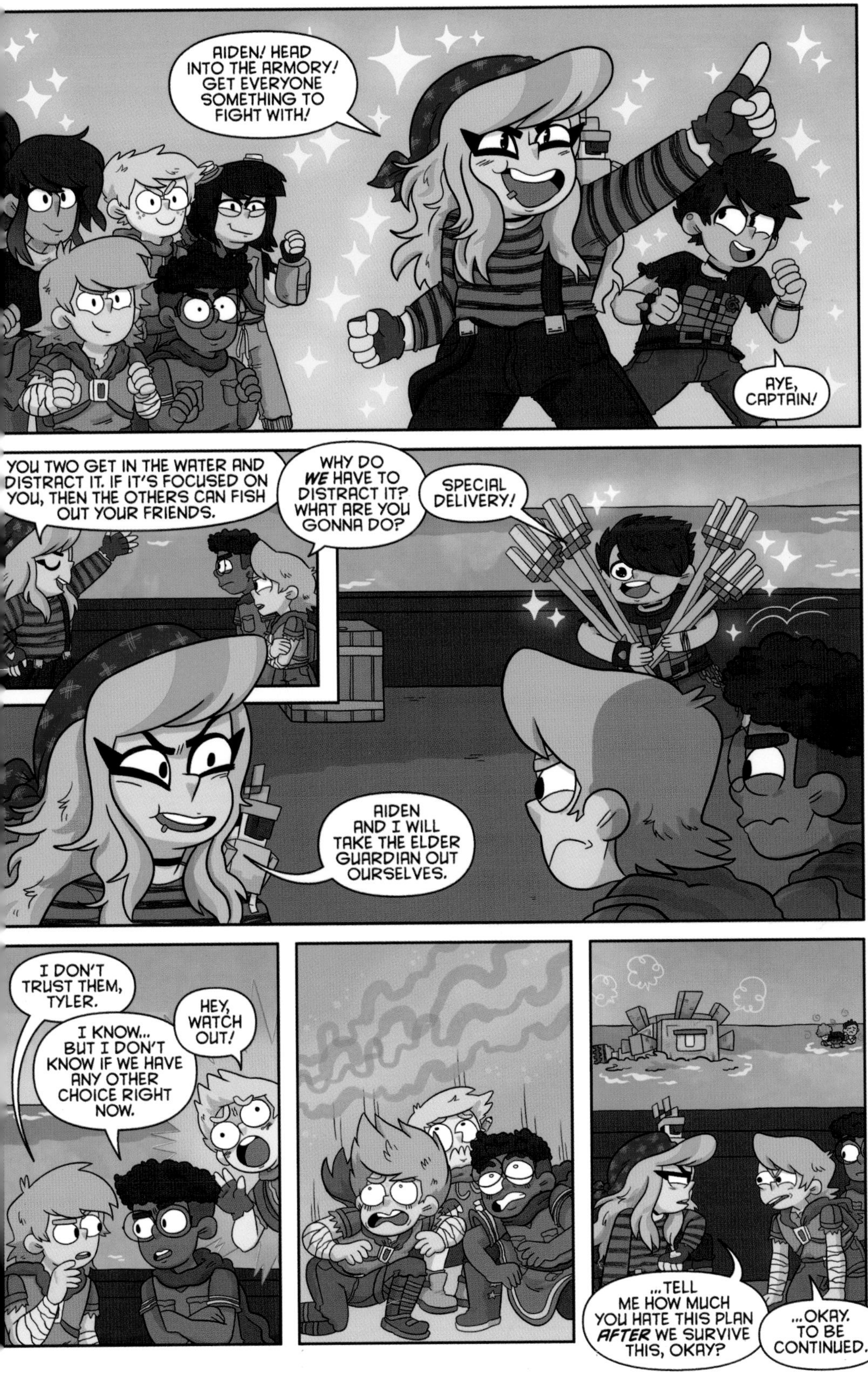

AIDEN! HEAD INTO THE ARMORY! GET EVERYONE SOMETHING TO FIGHT WITH!
AYE, CAPTAIN!
YOU TWO GET IN THE WATER AND DISTRACT IT. IF IT'S FOCUSED ON YOU, THEN THE OTHERS CAN FISH OUT YOUR FRIENDS.
WHY DO WE HAVE TO DISTRACT IT? WHAT ARE YOU GONNA DO?
SPECIAL DELIVERY!
AIDEN AND I WILL TAKE THE ELDER GUARDIAN OUT OURSELVES.
I DON'T TRUST THEM, TYLER.
I KNOW... BUT I DON'T KNOW IF WE HAVE ANY OTHER CHOICE RIGHT NOW.
HEY, WATCH OUT!
...TELL ME HOW MUCH YOU HATE THIS PLAN AFTER WE SURVIVE THIS, OKAY?
...OKAY.
TO BE CONTINUED.

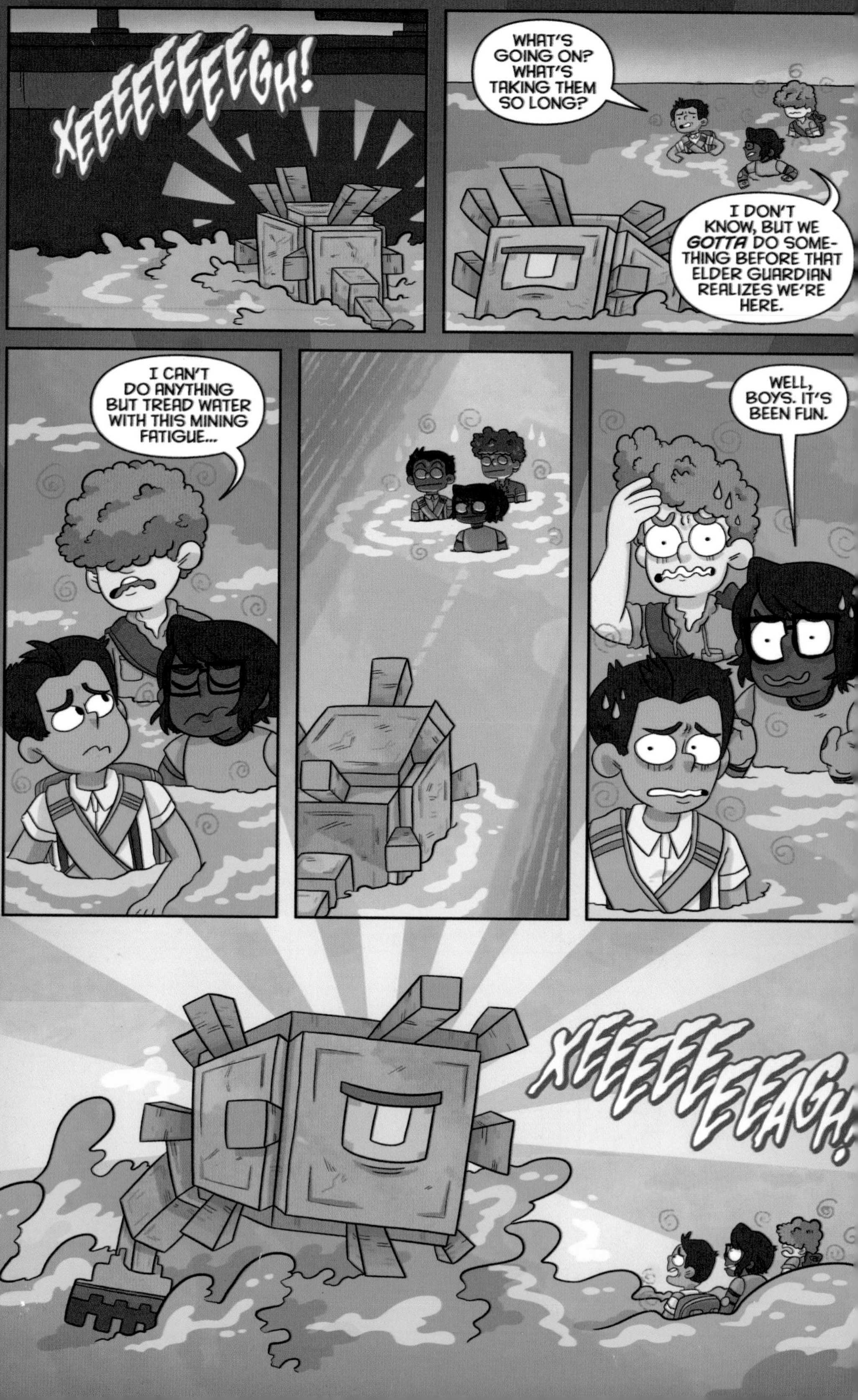
XEEEEEEEEEGH!
WHAT'S GOING ON? WHAT'S TAKING THEM SO LONG?
I DON'T KNOW, BUT WE GOTTA DO SOMETHING BEFORE THAT ELDER GUARDIAN REALIZES WE'RE HERE.
I CAN'T DO ANYTHING BUT TREAD WATER WITH THIS MINING FATIGUE...
WELL, BOYS. IT'S BEEN FUN.
XEEEEEEEAGH!

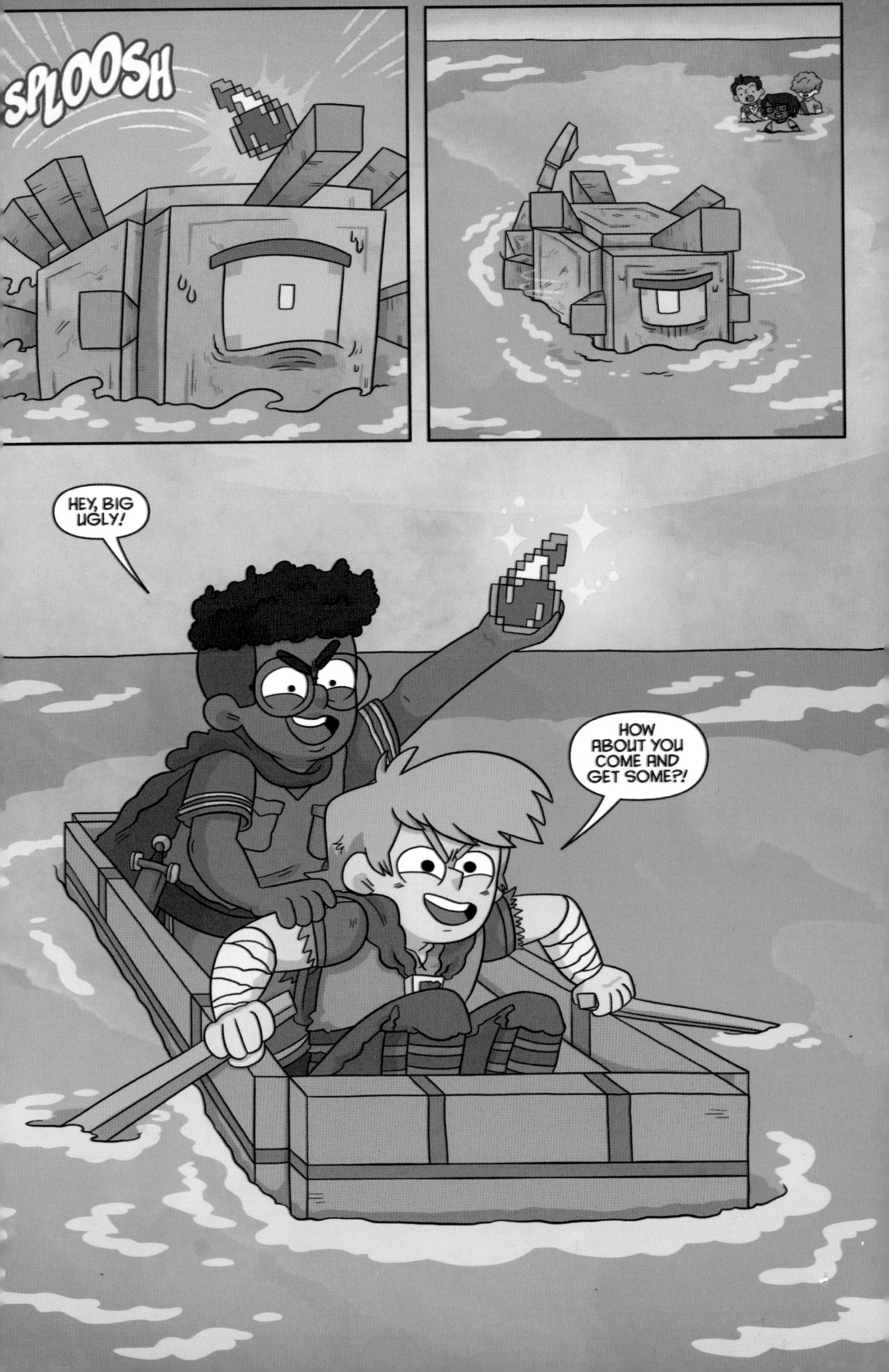
SPLOOSH
HEY, BIG UGLY!
HOW ABOUT YOU COME AND GET SOME?!

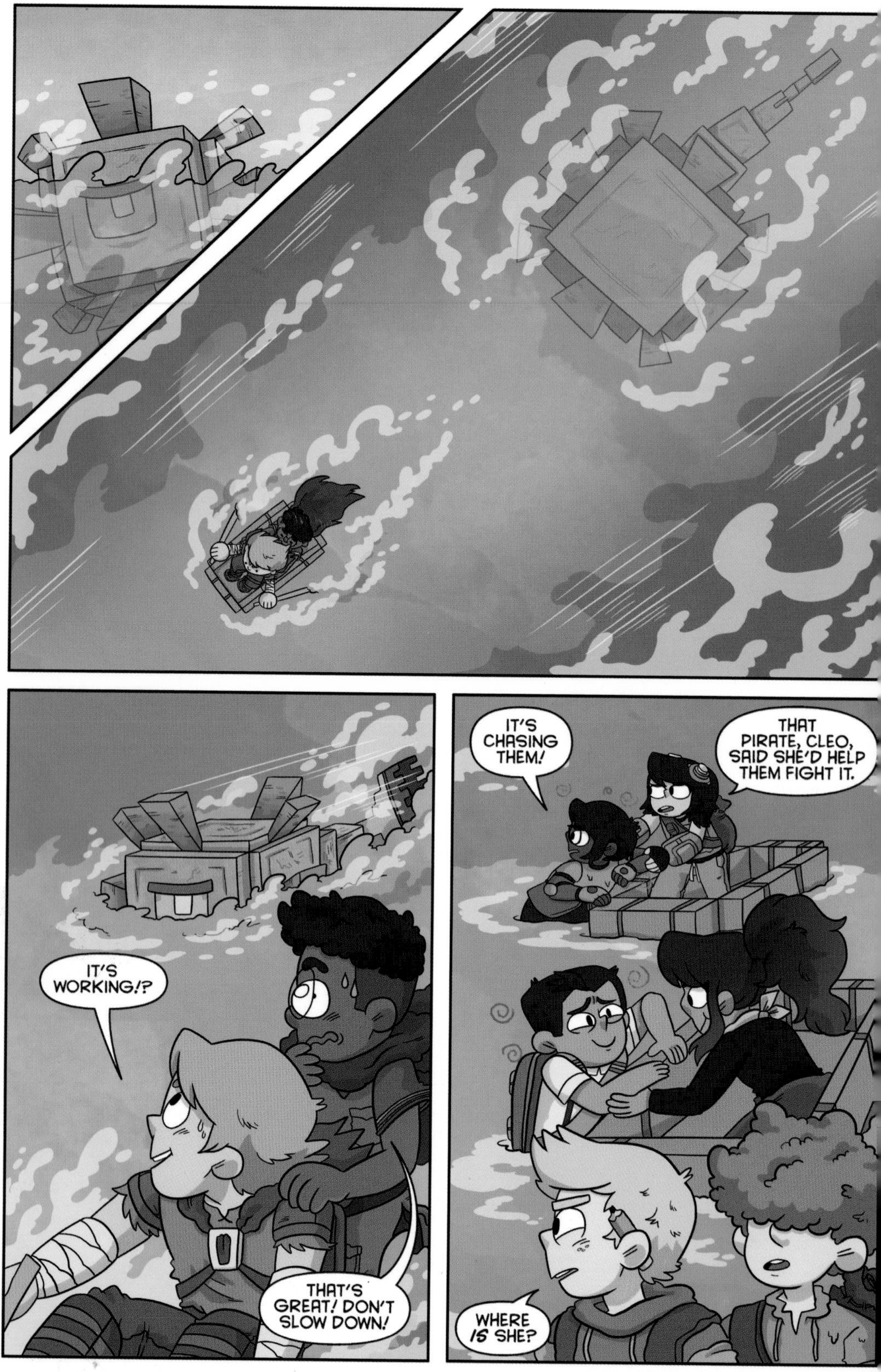
IT'S WORKING!?
THAT'S GREAT! DON'T SLOW DOWN!
IT'S CHASING THEM!
THAT PIRATE, CLEO, SAID SHE'D HELP THEM FIGHT IT.
WHERE IS SHE?

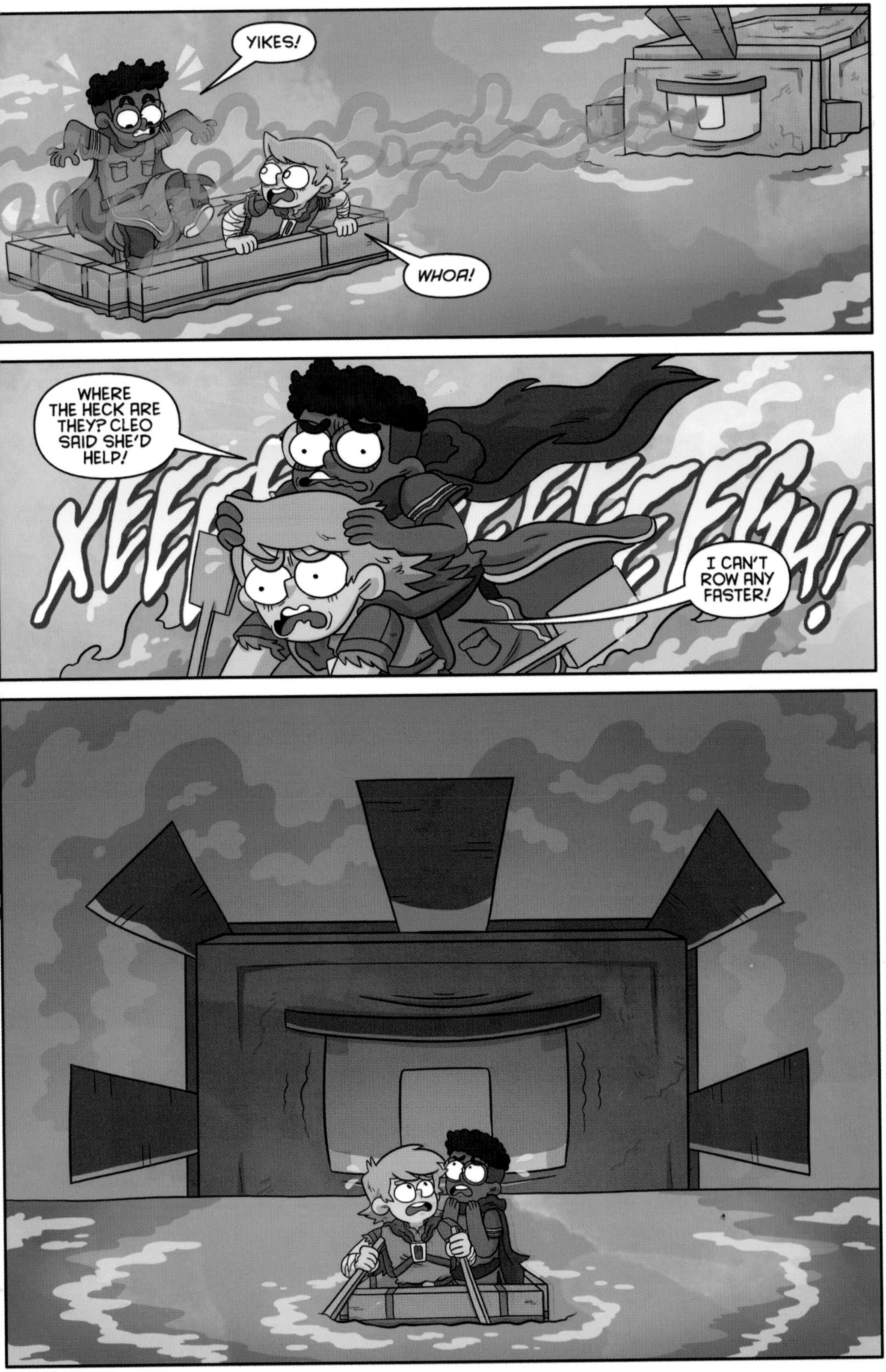
YIKES!
WHOA!
WHERE THE HECK ARE THEY? CLEO SAID SHE'D HELP!
I CAN'T ROW ANY FASTER!

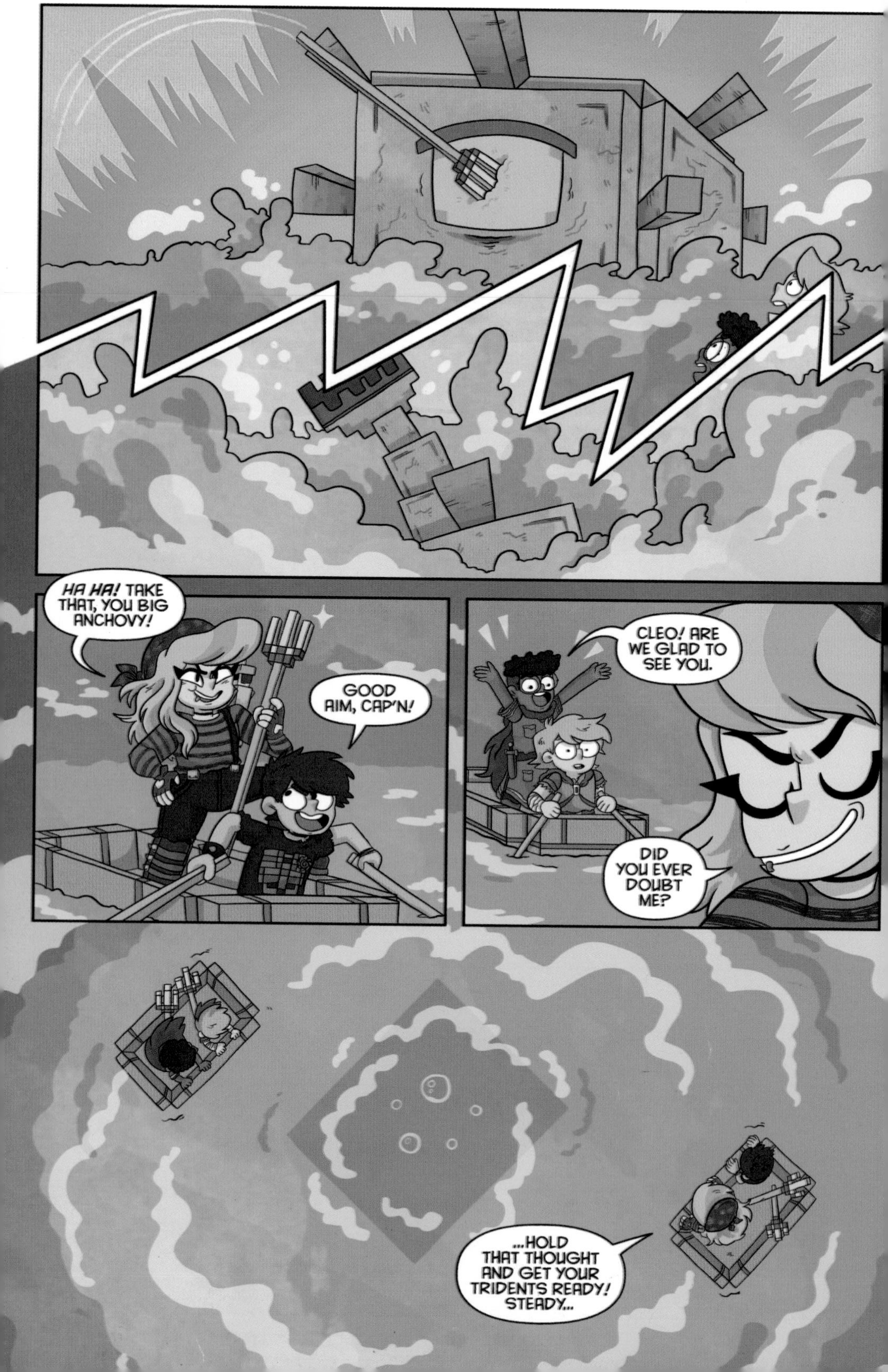
HA HA! TAKE THAT, YOU BIG ANCHOVY!
GOOD AIM, CAP'N!
CLEO! ARE WE GLAD TO SEE YOU.
DID YOU EVER DOUBT ME?
...HOLD THAT THOUGHT AND GET YOUR TRIDENTS READY! STEADY...

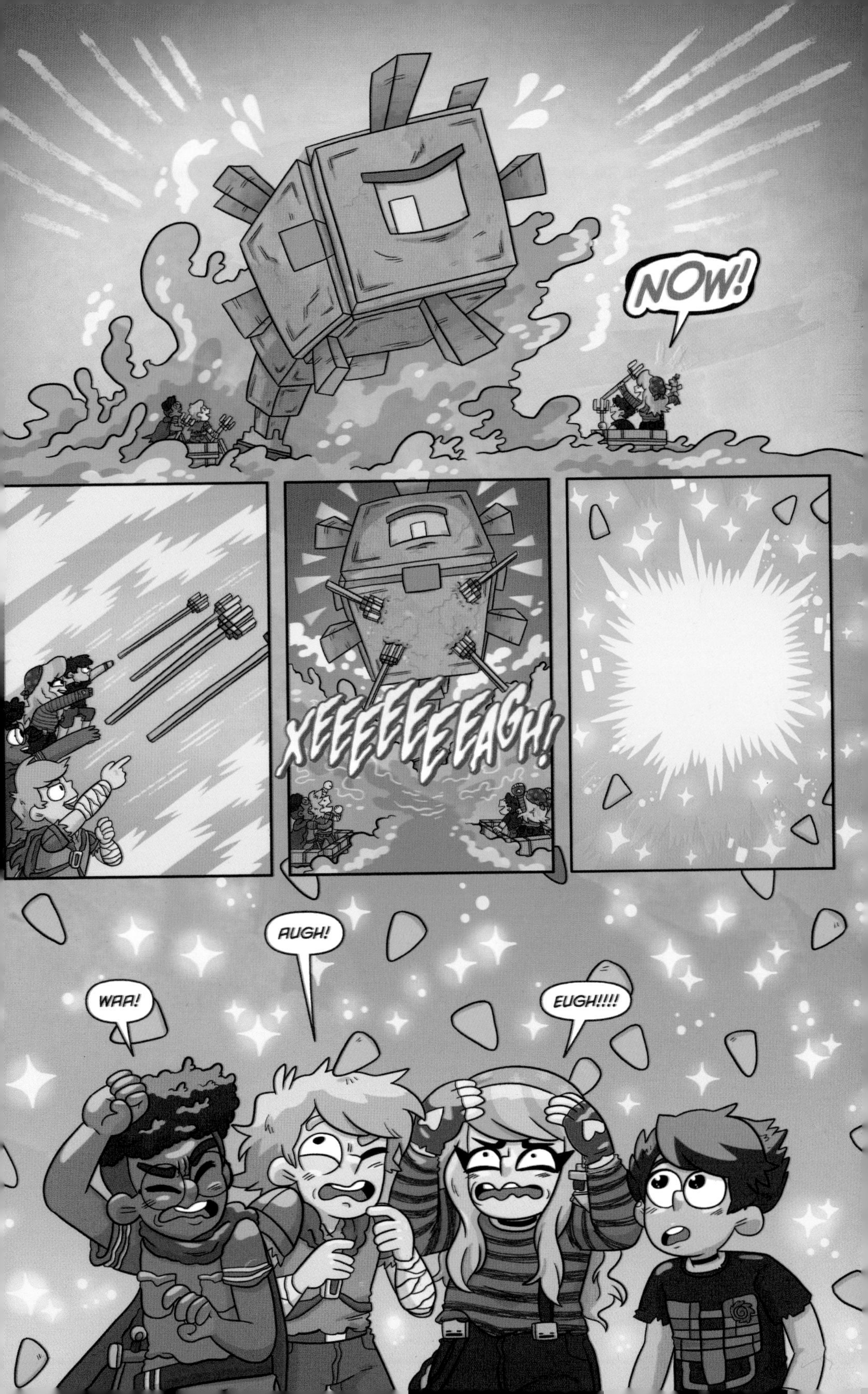
NOW!
XEEEEEEEAGH!
WAA!
AUGH!
EUGH!!!!

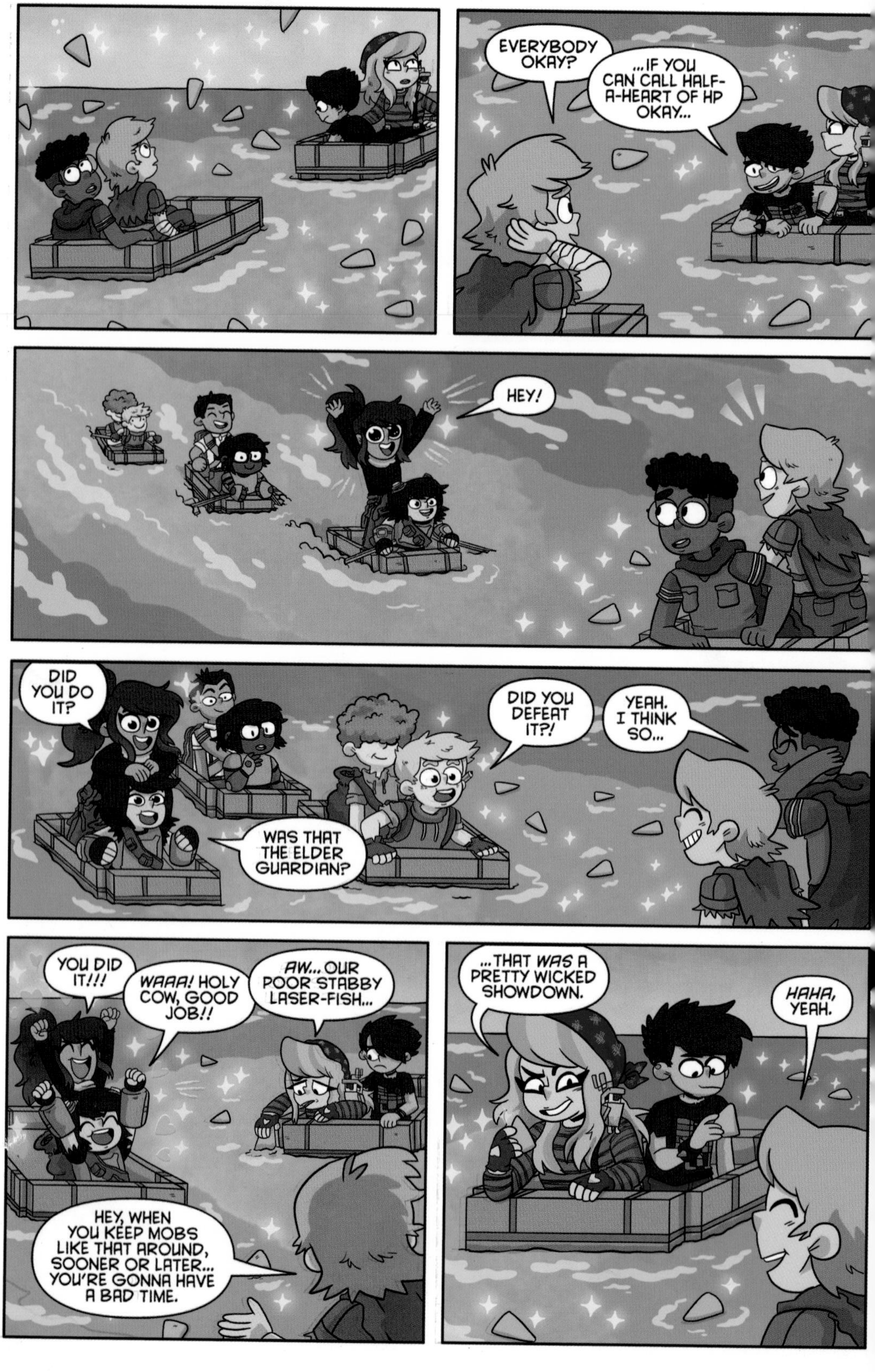
EVERYBODY OKAY?
...IF YOU CAN CALL HALF-A-HEART OF HP OKAY...
HEY!
DID YOU DO IT?
DID YOU DEFEAT IT?!
YEAH. I THINK SO...
WAS THAT THE ELDER GUARDIAN?
YOU DID IT!!!
WAAA! HOLY COW, GOOD JOB!!
AW... OUR POOR STABBY LASER-FISH...
HEY, WHEN YOU KEEP MOBS LIKE THAT AROUND, SOONER OR LATER... YOU'RE GONNA HAVE A BAD TIME.
...THAT WAS A PRETTY WICKED SHOWDOWN.
HAHA, YEAH.

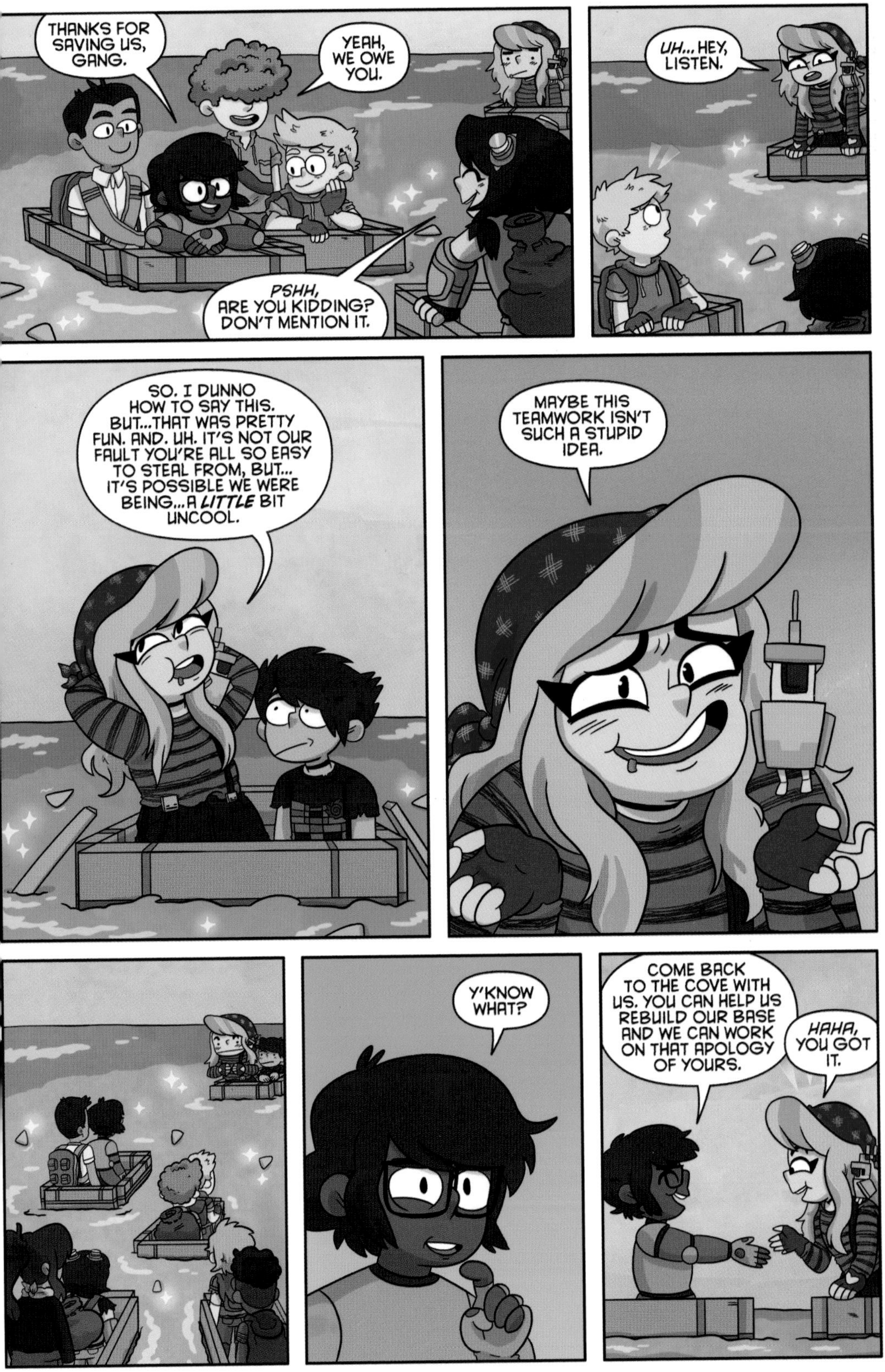
THANKS FOR SAVING US, GANG.
YEAH, WE OWE YOU.
PSHH, ARE YOU KIDDING? DON'T MENTION IT.
UH... HEY, LISTEN.
SO. I DUNNO HOW TO SAY THIS. BUT...THAT WAS PRETTY FUN. AND. UH. IT'S NOT OUR FAULT YOU'RE ALL SO EASY TO STEAL FROM, BUT... IT'S POSSIBLE WE WERE BEING...A LITTLE BIT UNCOOL.
MAYBE THIS TEAMWORK ISN'T SUCH A STUPID IDEA.
Y'KNOW WHAT?
COME BACK TO THE COVE WITH US. YOU CAN HELP US REBUILD OUR BASE AND WE CAN WORK ON THAT APOLOGY OF YOURS.
HAHA, YOU GOT IT.

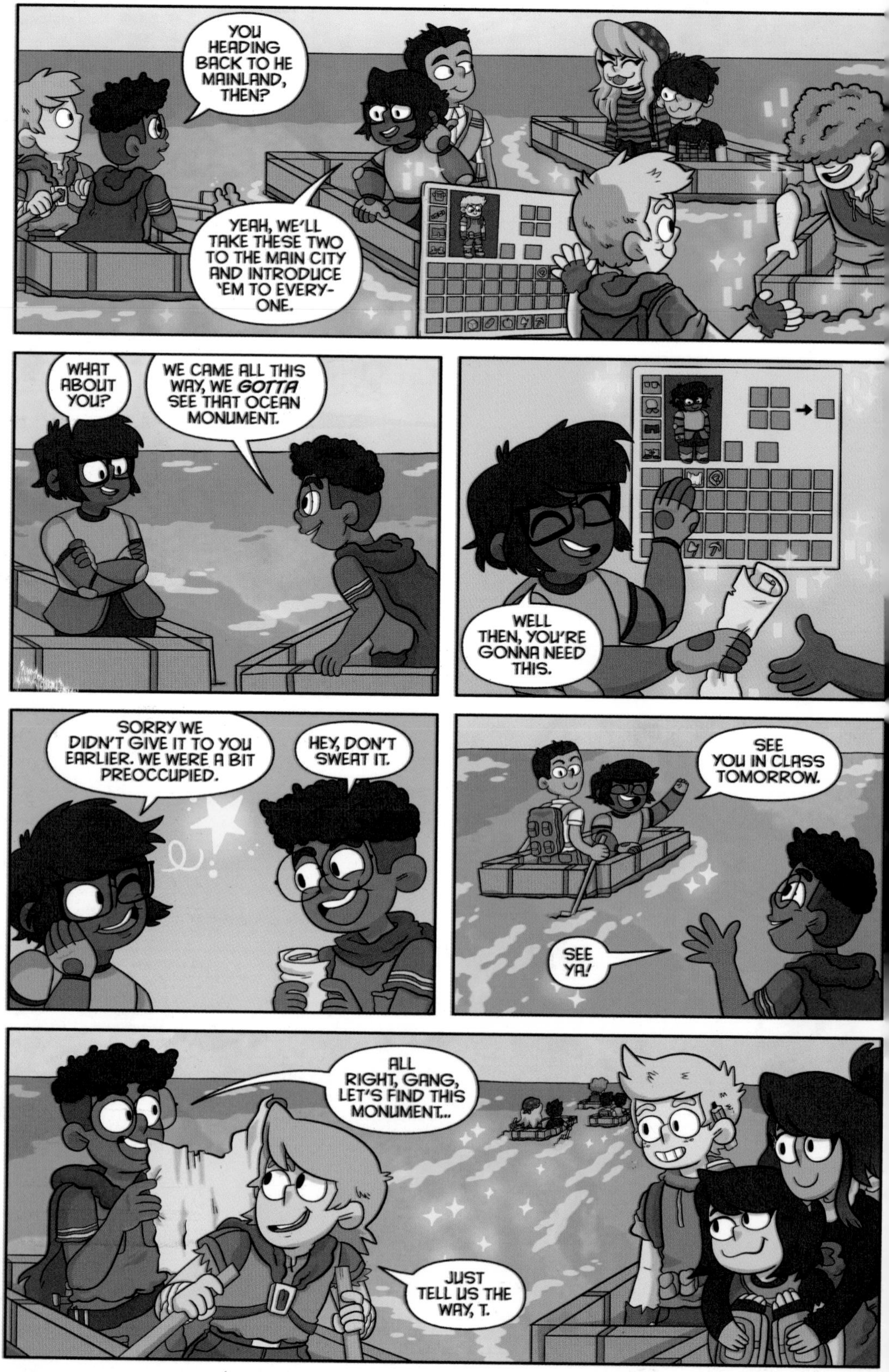

YOU HEADING BACK TO HE MAINLAND, THEN?
YEAH, WE'LL TAKE THESE TWO TO THE MAIN CITY AND INTRODUCE 'EM TO EVERY-ONE.
WHAT ABOUT YOU?
WE CAME ALL THIS WAY, WE *GOTTA* SEE THAT OCEAN MONUMENT.
WELL THEN, YOU'RE GONNA NEED THIS.
SORRY WE DIDN'T GIVE IT TO YOU EARLIER. WE WERE A BIT PREOCCUPIED.
HEY, DON'T SWEAT IT.
SEE YOU IN CLASS TOMORROW.
SEE YA!
ALL RIGHT, GANG, LET'S FIND THIS MONUMENT...
JUST TELL US THE WAY, T.

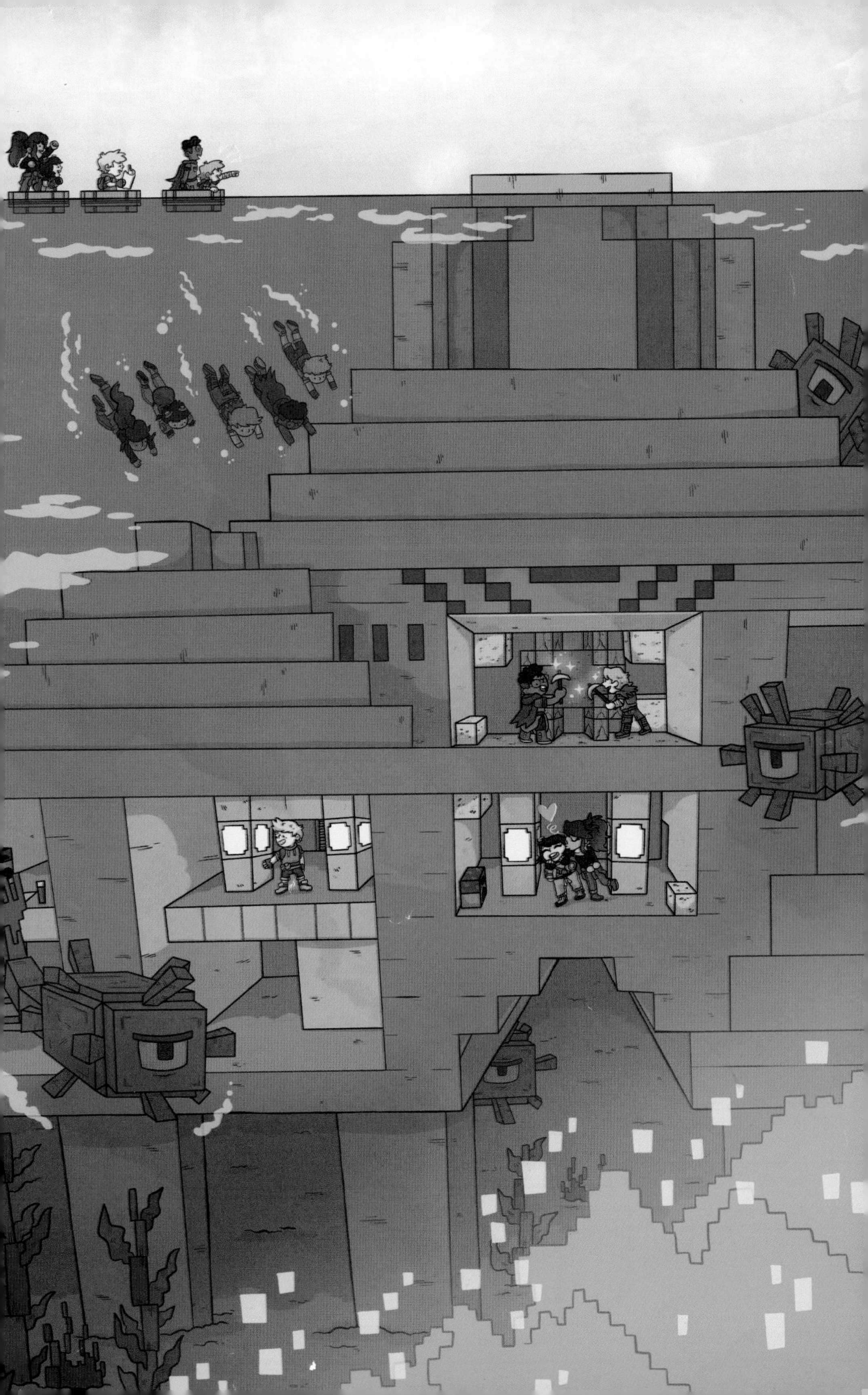

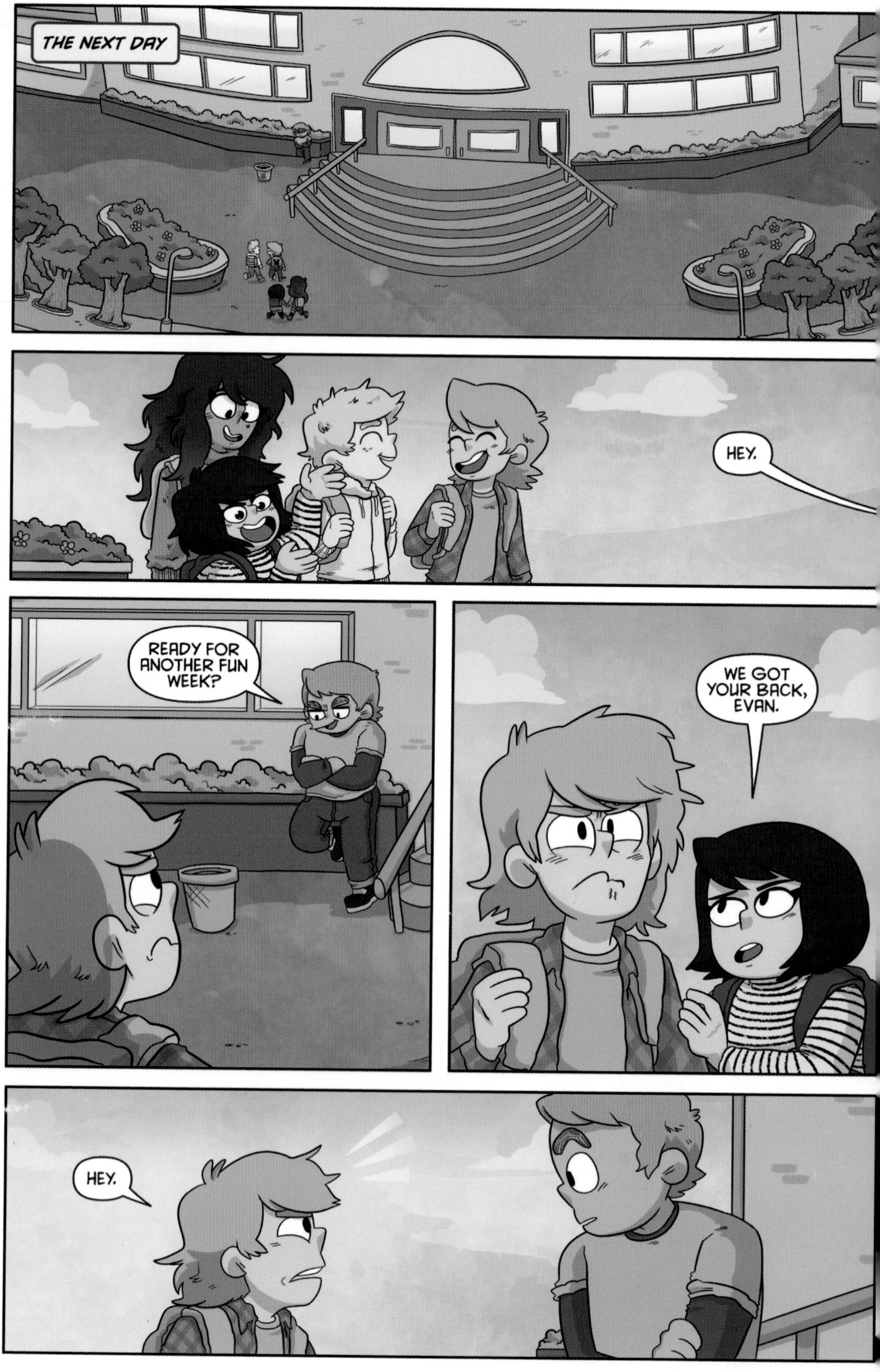
THE NEXT DAY
HEY.
READY FOR ANOTHER FUN WEEK?
WE GOT YOUR BACK, EVAN.
HEY.

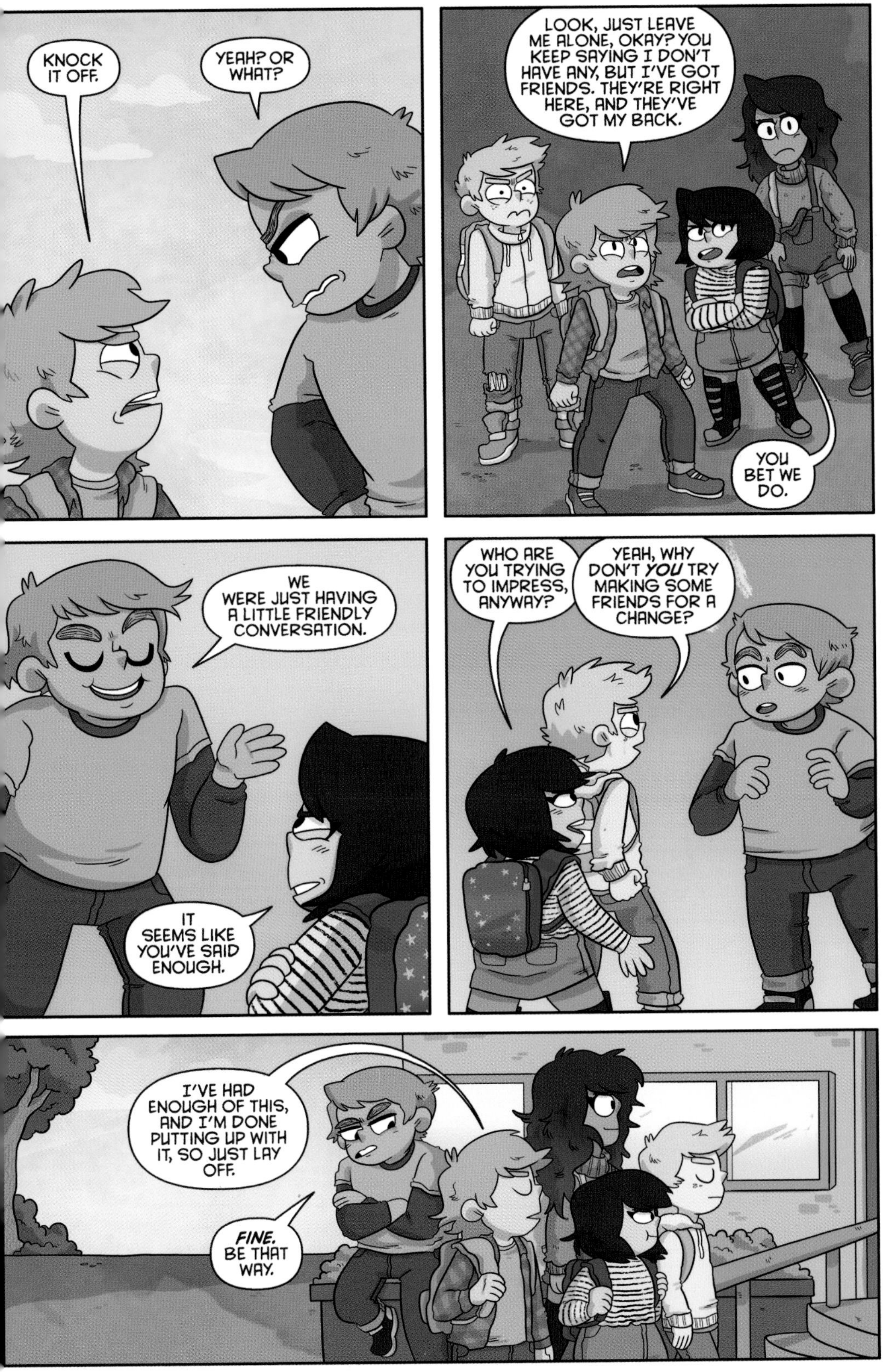
KNOCK IT OFF.
YEAH? OR WHAT?
LOOK, JUST LEAVE ME ALONE, OKAY? YOU KEEP SAYING I DON'T HAVE ANY, BUT I'VE GOT FRIENDS. THEY'RE RIGHT HERE, AND THEY'VE GOT MY BACK.
YOU BET WE DO.
WE WERE JUST HAVING A LITTLE FRIENDLY CONVERSATION.
IT SEEMS LIKE YOU'VE SAID ENOUGH.
WHO ARE YOU TRYING TO IMPRESS, ANYWAY?
YEAH, WHY DON'T ***YOU*** TRY MAKING SOME FRIENDS FOR A CHANGE?
I'VE HAD ENOUGH OF THIS, AND I'M DONE PUTTING UP WITH IT, SO JUST LAY OFF.
FINE. BE THAT WAY.

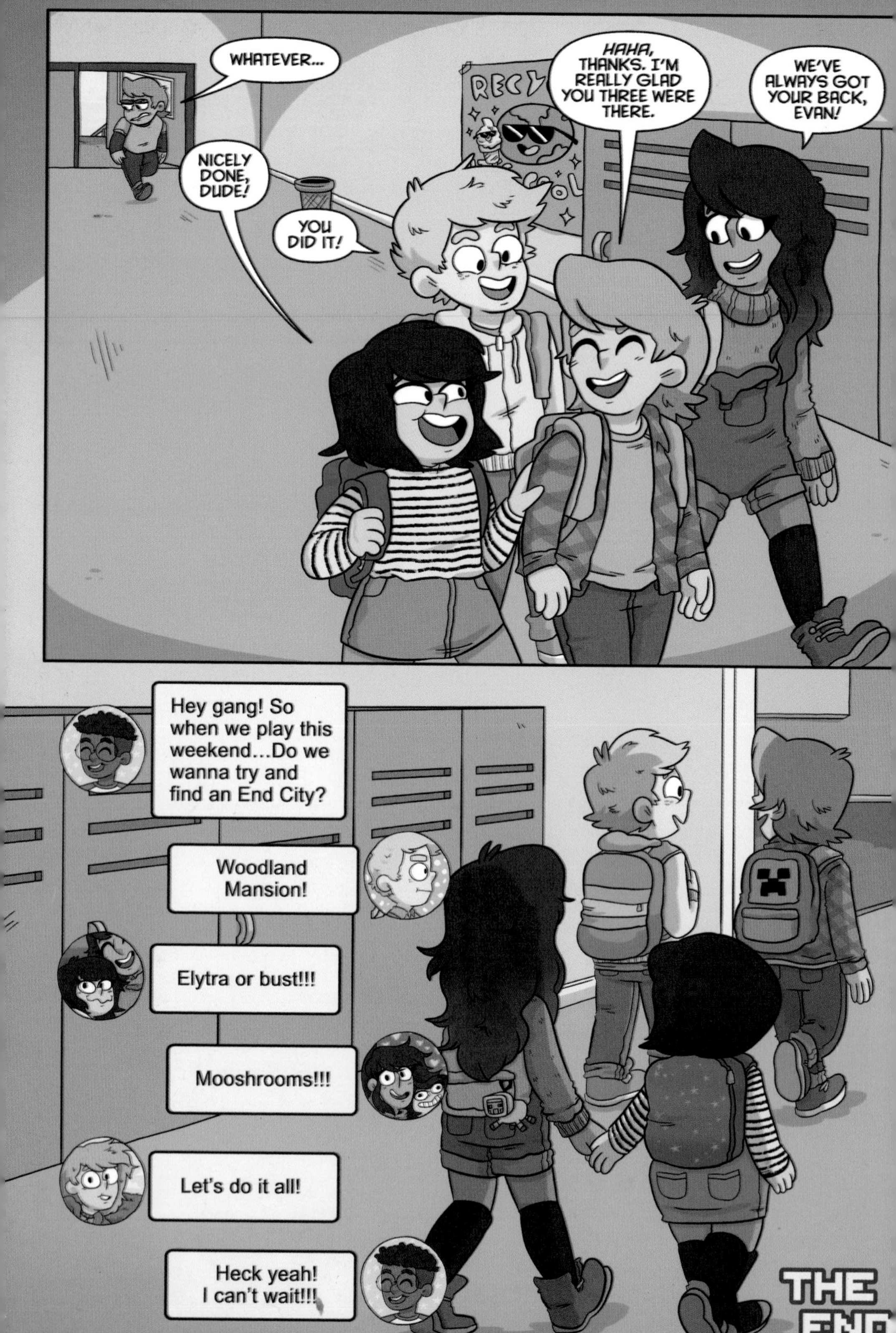
WHATEVER...
NICELY DONE, DUDE!
YOU DID IT!
HAHA, THANKS. I'M REALLY GLAD YOU THREE WERE THERE.
WE'VE ALWAYS GOT YOUR BACK, EVAN!
Hey gang! So when we play this weekend...Do we wanna try and find an End City?
Woodland Mansion!
Elytra or bust!!!
Mooshrooms!!!
Let's do it all!
Heck yeah! I can't wait!!!
THE END

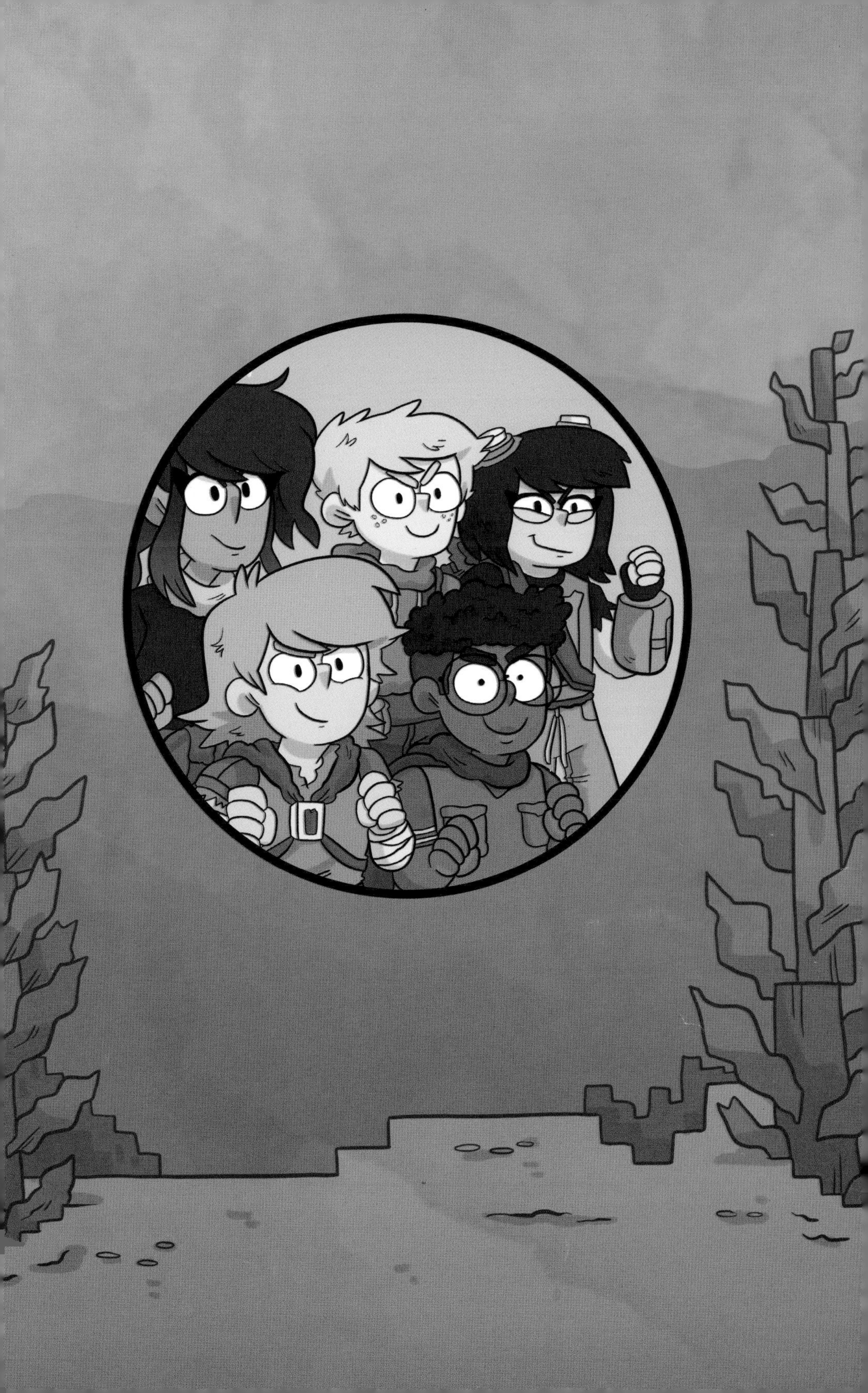

MINECRAFT™

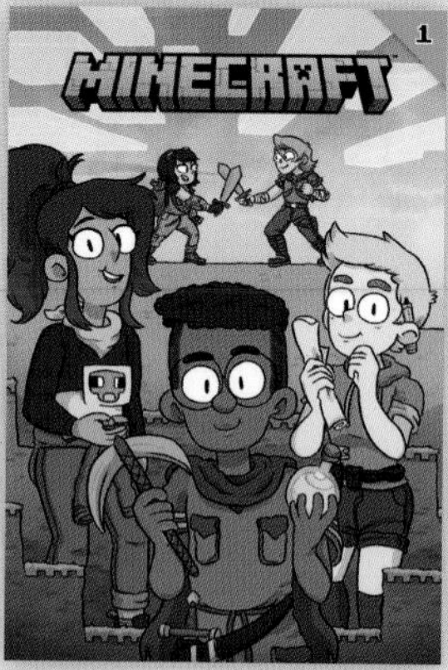
MINECRAFT
1

Hardcover Book ISBN
978-1-0982-5062-1

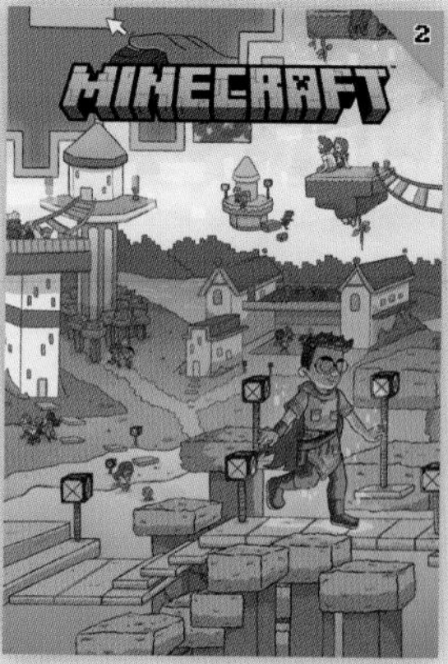
MINECRAFT
2

Hardcover Book ISBN
978-1-0982-5063-8

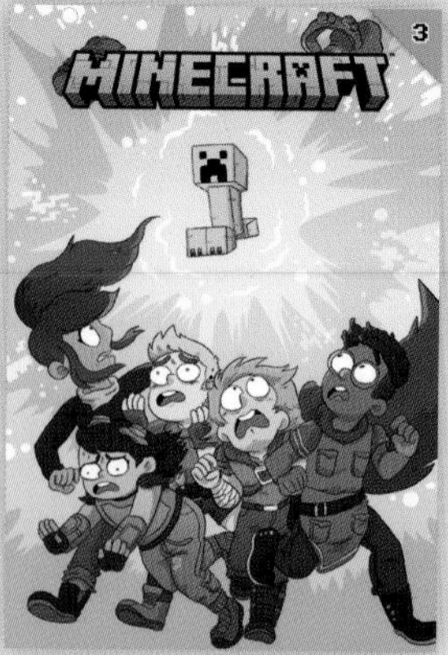
MINECRAFT
3

Hardcover Book ISBN
978-1-0982-5064-5

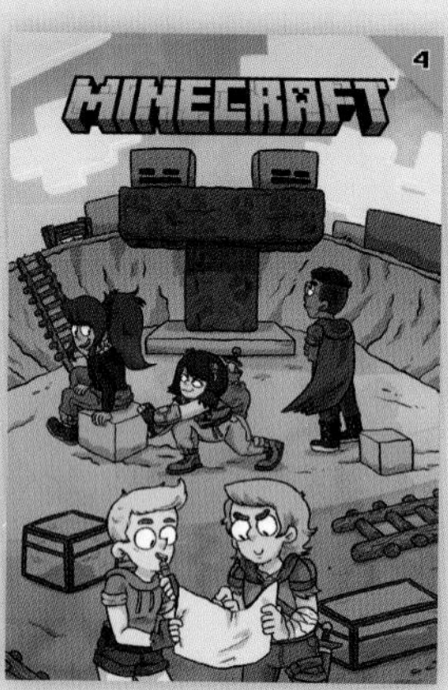
MINECRAFT
4

Hardcover Book ISBN
978-1-0982-5065-2

COLLECT THEM ALL!

**Set of 8 Hardcover Books ISBN:
978-1-0982-5061-4**

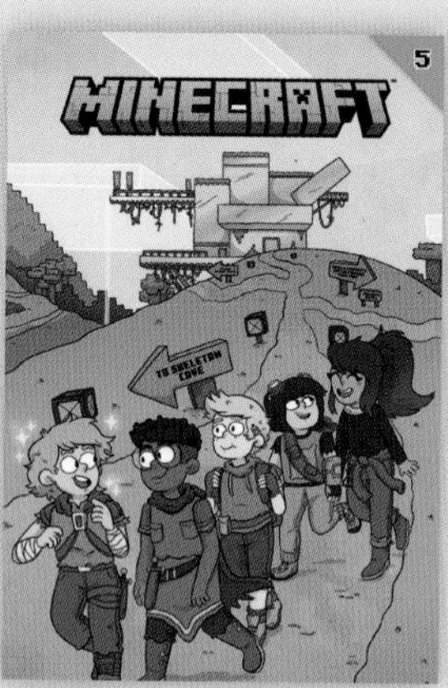
MINECRAFT
5

Hardcover Book ISBN
978-1-0982-5066-9

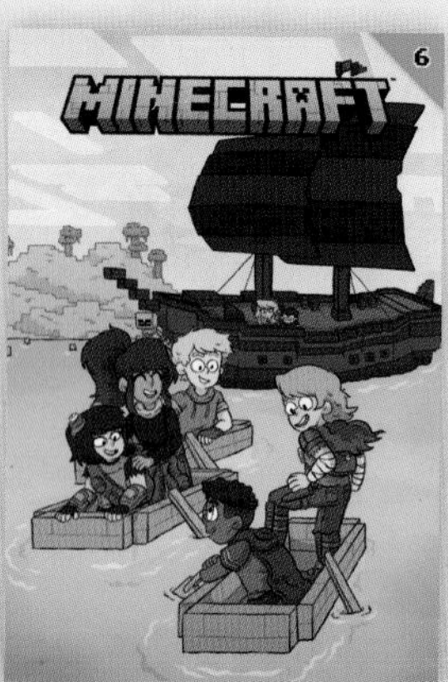
MINECRAFT
6

Hardcover Book ISBN
978-1-0982-5067-6

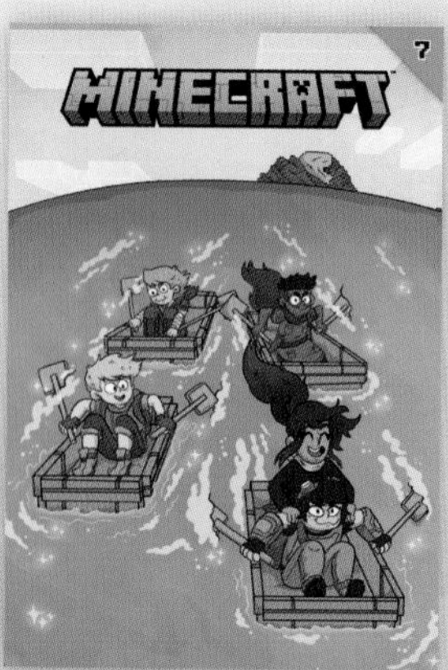
MINECRAFT
7

Hardcover Book ISBN
978-1-0982-5068-3

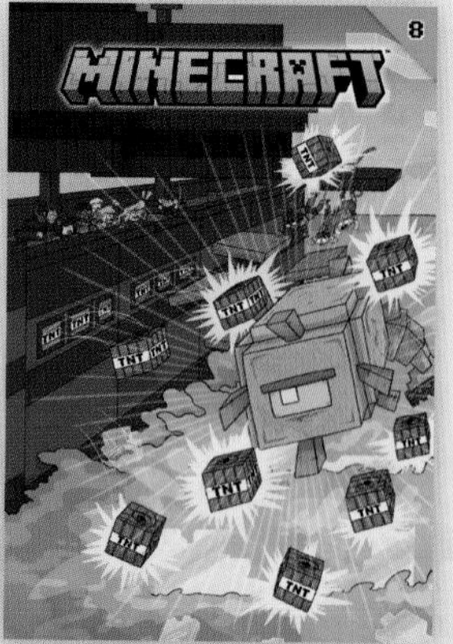
MINECRAFT
8

Hardcover Book ISBN
978-1-0982-5069-0